PINGO
the
PLAID PANDA

PINGO the PLAID PANDA

written and illustrated by
LOREEN LEEDY

HOLIDAY HOUSE · NEW YORK

For Jim *and* Patty

LIBRARY OF CONGRESS
Library of Congress Cataloging−in−Publication Data

Leedy, Loreen.
Pingo, the plaid panda / written and illustrated by Loreen Leedy.
—1st ed.
p. cm.
Summary: Convinced that the other pandas will not play with him
because he is plaid, Pingo takes steps to make himself look more
like them.
[1. Pandas—Fiction.   2. Self-acceptance—Fiction.]   I. Title.
PZ7.L51524Pi   1989
[E]—dc19   88-17005   CIP   AC

ISBN 0-8234-0727-6

Pingo was a panda, and he was plaid.
One day, he was singing, bop-a-dop,
and dancing, hop-a-lop!

Then he spotted some other pandas.
Pingo stared down at the ground and walked silently by.

"They don't like me because I'm plaid," he mumbled.
He plodded home alone.

"Pingo, what's the matter?" asked his mother.

"Mama, I'm plaid and I'm mad," he growled.

"There's nothing wrong with being plaid," Mama said. "Now go clean your room."

"Ugh," groaned Pingo.

He hung up his clothes, scooped up his shoes,
and picked up his toys, hop, hop, hop.
He unrolled his rug, untangled his sheets,

and unscrambled his socks, bop, bop, bop.
Then he stacked his books, fluffed his pillows,
and dumped his trash, plop, plop, plop.

"Whew!" Pingo was tired.

From outside came a whistling and a
tooting and a splashing.
It was Papa, playing with the hose.
Pingo ran out to talk to him.

"Papa, I'm plaid and I'm sad," sighed Pingo.
"The other pandas don't like me. I'm lonely."

"Son, we love you just the way you are,"
Papa said.

"But Papa . . ."

Mama was calling them to dinner,
so Papa and Pingo hurried into the house.

Pingo ate piles of potatoes and bunches
of beets, crunch, crunch.
He gobbled mounds of muffins and chunks
of cheese, munch, munch.

He nibbled morsels of melon and pieces of
pie, scrunch, scrunch.
Pingo was stuffed.

Papa said, "Let's clean up the kitchen."
Mama stacked the plates, scraped the pots,
and washed the dishes, clang, clang, clang.
Pingo wiped the table, swept the floor,

and pushed in the chairs, pang, pang, pang.
And Papa cleaned the stove, dried the dishes,
and dropped the potlids, bang, bang, bang!
The kitchen was clean.

Mama and Papa settled down
to read, think, and snooze.

But Pingo snuck into the bathroom,
and looked for Mama's black dye.
"I'll dye my plaid fur black," he thought,
"and then the other pandas will like me."

Pingo dripped and dribbled, plip, plip.
He sniffed and sneezed, zip, zip.
And when he looked in the mirror. . .
he wasn't plaid anymore.

Mama saw him and yelled,
"Pingo! You're not plaid, and I'm mad!"

He had to go to bed early that night.

The next morning, Pingo was happy and hopping.
He ran right up to the other pandas and smiled.

They all played ball, thump, thump.
They danced in circles, jump, jump.
And they turned somersaults, bump, bump.

The pandas said, "We're glad you played with us today, Pingo. We thought that you didn't like us."

"How did you know it was me?" asked Pingo.

"We could tell by your dancing," they replied.
"See you tomorrow."

Pingo scampered home.
"What happened?" asked Mama.

"The other pandas like me," explained Pingo.
"Being plaid has nothing to do with it."

Mama put Pingo in the bathtub to wash out the black hair dye.

She soaked and scrubbed, blub, blub.
She rinsed and rubbed, dub, dub.
She dried and puffed and fluffed him,
until he looked like himself again.

Pingo jumped into the air and shouted,
"I'm plaid and I'm glad!"